This book belongs to

Printed in the U.S.A.

ISBN 0-7172-8282-1
Previously published as 0-681-40869-3

Jim Henson's Muppet Babies
Head to Toe

by Bonnie Worth   illustrated by Kathy Spahr

Your head holds your brain,
And your brain is for thinking.

$E = mc^2$
$2 + 2 = 4$

Your eyes are for seeing
And crying and blinking.

Your ears are for hearing,
Your nose is for sneezing,

Your lips are for kissing,
Your cheeks are for squeezing.

Your tongue is for talking

And tasting and licking.

Your teeth are for chewing

And brushing and clicking.

Your elbows, your shoulders,
Wrists, ankles, and knees
Are hinges to help you
To bend as you please.

With legs you can walk,
You can skip, you can play.
With legs you can really
Get carried away!

Your arms are to hug
And to climb and to throw,

To lift and to hold,
To swing high and low.

Your hair is to warm you,
To wash and shampoo.

It's curly or straight—
Just what sort have you?

And everyone knows
That the purpose of skin
Is to keep all the things
That are inside you in.

Take a look at the colors
That skin can come in!

Your feet keep your balance—
Your toes do that, too.

They sometimes are ticklish.
How ticklish are you?

Your hands are to wave
And to juggle and clap,
And also to fold
And to rest in your lap.

With fingers you paint
And you draw and you touch.
With fingers you can do—
Oh, ever so much!

So now that you've learned
All the parts, large and small,
Just take out your pointer
And point to them all!

teeth

toe

ankle

foot

leg

knee